BOOKS BY LAURA (L.A.)MARIANI

Untamed Hearts

The BAD Boy

The BAD Girl

Holiday Romance

14 Days to Love Series: Short Sweet Steamy

Parisian Serendipity

Venetian Whispers

Mumbay Surprise

Romeo in Rome

New York Melody

Artic Embrace

Santorini Sunsets

Havana Heat

Barcelona Dreams

Marrakesh Magic

Vienna Waltz

Sydney Sparks

Amsterdam Affair

Cape Town Safari

Box Set

14 Days to Love: Short Sweet Steamy

Twelve Days of Christmas Series

A Partridge in a Pear Tree: Hot Spicy Christmas Novella

Two Turtle Doves: Hot Spicy Christmas Novella

Three French Hens: Hot Spicy Christmas Novella

Four Calling Birds: Hot Spicy Christmas Novella

Five Golden Rings: Hot Spicy Christmas Novella

Six Geese a-Laying: Hot Spicy Christmas Novella

Seven Swans a-Swimming: Hot Spicy Christmas Novella

Eight Maids a-Milking: Hot Spicy Christmas Novella

Nine Ladies Dancing: Hot Spicy Christmas Novella

Ten Lords a-Leaping: Hot Spicy Christmas Novella

Eleven Pipers Piping: Hot Spicy Christmas Novella

Twelve Drummers Drumming: Hot Spicy Christmas Novella

Box Set

Twelve Days of Christmas

Shadowbrook Paranormal Series

A Halloween Romance: Enchanted in Shadowbrook

The Midnight Hour: A Halloween Shadowbrook Romance

Navy Seals Hunks Series

SEALed Hearts

SEALed with a Kiss

SEALed Undercover

SEALed Pursuit

SEALed Love Code

SEALed beyond Duty

Box Set

Navy SEAL Hunks

A Royal Romance Trilogy

A Coronation Weekend Romance

The Wicked Princess

The Lost Kingdom

Box Set

A Royal RomanceTrilogy

The Nine Lives of Gabrielle Series

Gabrielle (prequel/first in series)

For Three She Plays

A New York Adventure

Searching for Goren

Tasting Freedom

For Three She Strays

Paris Toujours Paris

Me Myself and Us

Freedom Over Me

For Three She Stays

London Calling

Back in Your Arms

The Greatest Love

Box Sets

For Three She Plays - Book 1-3

For Three She Strays - Book 4-6

For Three She Stays - Book 7-9

The Nine Lives of Gabrielle Book 1-9 + 3 Bonus stories

Box Set - Italian Edition

Le Nove Vite di Gabrielle: Libri 1-9 + 3 Bonus

THE BAD GIRL

UNTAMED HEARTS
BOOK 2

LAURA (L.A.) MARIANI

ISBN: 978-1-917104-17-3

FOREWORD

The Bad Girl is a OTT insta-love steamy romance novella that is intended for a mature audience. If you crave a fast-paced, passionate read, jump right in!

Previous in the series - **The Bad Boy.**

PROLOGUE

I stand tall, my six-inch stilettos clicking against the marble floor of my penthouse apartment. My perfectly manicured fingers brush away a strand of long red hair that has fallen into my emerald eyes. I take a sip of scotch and gaze out at the city below, the windows offering a dazzling view of towering skyscrapers and bustling streets. It's taken years of hard work and determination to reach this level of success in the male-dominated tech industry. And tomorrow, I will solidify my place as a leader by delivering the keynote speech at the annual conference. A smirk plays on my lips as I think about proving all those who doubted me wrong. A frown creases my perfect red lips as I think about the additional security measure the board has forced upon me: hiring someone for my personal protection. It reeks of paranoia and sexism as if they believe a woman can't fend for herself in this cutthroat world.

I glance at the vintage grandfather clock in the corner, its incessant ticking echoing through the empty room. My restless footsteps pace across the hardwood floor as I remember last night visitor, the desperate need for submission fueling my disdain. I sneer, remembering the feeble attempts to please me, his surrender coming too quickly. Frustrated, I turn away from the window, my designer heels clicking loudly with every step. My thoughts race with final edits; I mull over every word and inflection of the upcoming speech, my mind buzzing with last-minute edits and revisions.

"Mistress," faint sobs begging for mercy in the background. "Mistress," he called me, and I laughed coldly, feeding off his humiliation.

The thought of being in that vulnerable position again makes my core clench, but I quickly push it away; I am in control now. No man will ever have power over me again - I've worked too hard and sacrificed too much to let that happen.

Tomorrow, everyone will know, and I will cement my place at the top of the food chain—alpha female in a sea of beta sharks. I will deliver a speech that will leave them all in awe, and if it means swallowing my pride and dealing with a personal bodyguard, so be it.

My mind buzzes with anticipation for tomorrow as I lay in bed wishing for some rest but, lurking beneath the surface, I can't help but feel a simmering yearning desire for something more.

1

RED

J ohn's finger traces the rim of his glass, leaving a trail in the condensation. "How long has it been?" he asks as I pour him a generous scotch.

"Since when?" I reply, leaning against the bar.

"Since you left the Service," John says, his voice heavy with nostalgia. He takes a sip and grimaces at the taste.

I sip my drink and sigh, "Ten years, more or less." It feels like a lifetime ago, but also just yesterday.

"You done good, brother." John's expression softens as he speaks. We have both come a long way since our days in the military. Reed Enterprises has become one of the most respected security firms worldwide, known only to those who need its services. "I can't complain," I say, raising my glass to toast.

John leans in closer. "All good for the job?"

I furrow my brow. "Pardon?"

"Olivia Hunter?"

I nod, understanding now. "Oh yes, my men are all set, don't worry."

John shakes his head and leans in closer. "No, no, I really need YOU to look after her."

I frown, not wanting to get involved in any pseudo-celebrity protection gig. "They are all trained, ex-forces... I don't do personal bodyguarding to spoiled little madams..."

"I know, but I need someone I can trust. You owe me," John continues, his tone pleading now.

"Oh, common, how long will you keep using that same old story?" He is right, though. I owe him. After all, it was him and his team of SEALs who saved my men and me during our last mission.

. . .

"There have been threats to her life. Letters. From many different sources, some are scrawled , some typed, and some assembled from cutouts ..."

"I heard she's one hell of an insufferable bitch," I scoff.

"Perhaps ... but she is great at her job and that's all the Board cares about," John declares.

"She treats men like shit."

"Weak men," John smirks, "My oh my, are you scared she will boss you around and tame you?"

"Behave!"

"You are ever so British ..."

"Well, I can't help it," I say with a wink before I raise my glass and take another sip. "God save the King!"

———

I stand at the back of the crowded conference hall, my eyes locked on the stunning redhead commanding the stage. Olivia Hunter, tech queen and corporate powerhouse. Her fiery hair cascades over her shoulders, and her hourglass figure is poured into a skin-tight red dress. Those piercing green eyes scan the audience as she launches her keynote speech.

"Innovation. Disruption. Those aren't just buzzwords; they're the lifeblood of success in this industry." Her voice is pure sex and authority. She owns every man in this room, and she knows it.

My pulse races as I watch her, imagining that lush, curvy body writhing under me, those plump red lips parted in ecstasy. I want to grab fistfuls of that silky hair as I bend her over the podium and fuck her in front of everyone. Fuck me, her arrogance turns me on.

She meets my heated gaze, a spark of interest flaring in those emerald depths before she looks away. But I caught it. She felt that primal pull, too, the urge to dominate and possess. To battle for control.

I adjust my hardening cock, barely hearing her words over the pounding of my own heart. This powerful woman is used to men bowing before her. I want her begging for my cock, submitting to my will.

Eventually.

· · ·

Right now, I have a job to do. The conference attendees applaud as Olivia concludes her electrifying speech. She nods graciously, a slow smile playing at the corners of her mouth. Then her eyes find me again and narrow slightly. A challenge. Game on, Red.

"Mr Reed," her voice low and controlled, "I understand you're here to protect me, but I need you to be invisible," she says, gesturing me away to the background.

"I'm here to do a job, Ms. Hunter," my jaw clenched and my eyes fixed on her. "Whichever way I see fit."

"I am in charge," she retorts, tapping a manicured nail on her desk. "You work for me."

Bitch. "I do not, and until the threat is neutralized, you'll have to get used to having someone looking out for you."

"Then get me a drink," she dismisses me with a wave, her chair screeching against the floor.

"I am here to protect, not to serve," my voice now dripping with barely veiled contempt, "get it yourself."

"Isn't that what your kind does? Serve queens …?"

. . .

"I've served THE Queen, not any deluded queen." Ignorant bitch. "I'm not here to debate Red. I'm here to keep you safe, whether you like it or not." Her emerald green eyes narrow with disgust, her jaw set in a firm line as she stands tall, hands clenched into fists at her sides.

"I've dealt with far worse than some faceless threat," she spits out, her voice laced with contempt. "I don't need your help. Get the hell out of here," she screams, throwing a glass at me in frustration. As the tumbler shatters against the wall behind me, time seems to slow down, and the tension between us thickens.

Without thinking, I grab her by the arms and pull her close to me in one swift motion. I can feel the heat emanating from her body. She moans, her body betraying her as it presses against mine. I want to pull her over my knee and teach her a lesson, show her who's in charge.

Shit, shit, shit.

I pull back, my breathing ragged, "I'm sorry," I breathe. "I shouldn't have done that."

We stare at each other for a moment longer before Olivia wrenches herself out of my grasp and rushes out, her cheeks flushed . "Damn it," I curse under my breath as she disappears down the hallway. I lost control.

2

A CHINK IN THE ARMOR

The crowd applauds. But I don't care about their applause. My green eyes zero in on a man I've never laid eyes on before. My bodyguard. His presence commands attention, even in a sea of suits. He's tall, with a broad chin and a chiseled jawline. He's not the only one staring, but I feel like he's the only one who sees me—the real me, not the CEO persona I always wear like armor.

My heart is racing; I need to quench the fire he's ignited within me. I make my way to the back, but he's there, leaning against the wall with a smirk that makes my pussy clench. His eyes rake over my curves, and I resist the urge to squirm under his intense gaze. No man has ever affected me like this. I can't let it control me. I can't let any man ...

"Fetch me a drink," I order him. I reluctantly agreed to have a bodyguard, but it is going to be on my terms, as it always is.

. . .

"Get it yourself," he growls, his breath dancing over my ear, sending shivers down my spine.

I whirl around, my fists on my hips, attempting to regain the upper hand. "Who do you think you are, coming in here and talking to me like that?" Before I know it, I have thrown a glass at him in frustration. As the tumbler shatters against the wall he is standing over me, grabbing my wrists. He is soo close, I fight to keep control but my body betrays me, melting into him, eager for more. His grip on my wrist tightens as if to remind me who's in charge. The fire within me rages, combating with the last shreds of my willpower. Fuck you!

"Sorry," he says as he pulls back. I wanted him to explore every inch of my mouth. I run down the hallway, and my insides are in knots. Today, for the first time in a long time, I am not in control—and I liked it.

3

CLEAR AND PRESENT DANGER

I stride into Olivia's office, my boots thudding against the hardwood floor. My eyes immediately lock onto her fierce green gaze, the color blazing with a mixture of defiance and desire. "We need to talk," I growl.

She arches a perfectly sculpted brow, a hint of amusement playing on her full lips." Is that so? I wasn't aware we had anything to discuss, Mr. Reed."

The way my name rolls off her tongue sends a jolt of heat straight to my groin, and I clench my jaw, fighting the urge to throw her against the wall and show her exactly who's in charge.

"Cut the crap, Olivia. I'm your shadow, whether you like it or not." I step closer, invading her space and ignoring the intoxicating scent of her perfume that wraps around me like a vice.

. . .

Her dismissive tone only fuels my frustration. "Listen, this whole thing is John's idea... "she continues, crossing her arms over her chest. "This sudden obsession with protecting me. I'm willing to go along for now, but let's be clear. I won't let this alter my life one little bit."

My blood boils at her dismissive tone. Images of her lush curves writhing beneath me flood my mind. I want to break that icy exterior, make her beg for my touch. She doesn't know about the letters or the black Toyota 4X4 that has been following us for the last few days.

"I don't want you to do anything you've always done," I continue unperturbed.

She scoffs and mimics me, "Don't want me doing what I've always done? You're insane."

"Tough shit, sweetheart." I grin. "You're stuck with me."

Just then, Gert burst into the room. "Ms. Hunter, we have a major security breach. The servers are down." It isn't just random letters and potential attacks anymore; someone is deliberately targeting Olivia and her company, trying to sabotage them.

. . .

Olivia's eyes narrow to slits as she glares at me. Before she can retort, a loud crash echoes from the hallway. My instincts kick in, and I lunge towards her, pushing her to the ground just as bullets shatter the window behind her desk.

Glass shards rain down around us as I shield her trembling body with my own. "Fuck," I mutter against her neck, feeling the softness of her skin under my lips. She gazes up at me with fear and grudging respect.

"What the hell is going on?" she yells, confusion evident in her voice.

I brush a strand of fiery hair from her face, my fingers lingering on her skin. "I don't know, but I'm sure as hell going to find out. And until I do..." I pull her closer to me, my hand fisting in her hair. She melts into my embrace, her nails digging into my biceps. "Until then, I'll keep you safe, Red. Even if it means tying you to my bed," I whisper fiercely.

This isn't over yet. But one thing is sure - no one threatens what is mine.

4

A SNAKE AMONGST US

With a fierce grip on her wrist, I pull Olivia through the maze of Hunter Enterprises. My heart pounds in my chest as we approach our destination.

"Keep up," I command, glancing over my shoulder to make sure she's still with me. Her heels clack against the marble floor as she struggles to match my pace. "We're ending this now." I know now.

She doesn't argue, doesn't fight. It's a dance we've started—me leading, her following—and the power shift thrills me more than I expected. My dominant grip on her arm isn't just guiding; it's claiming, owning.

"Where are we going?" Her voice is breathless, a mix of adrenaline and something else—a quiver of submission that sends heat straight to my groin.

• • •

"To confront the traitor," I growl, not looking back at her. We finally reach the office where I've traced the leak in her company, the one selling her secrets and trying to kill us both. I kick open the door, relishing seeing fear etched across the traitor's face as they crouch in their chair.

"Everyone out," I command, pointing to everyone except the guilty party. They scatter, leaving behind a trail of nervous glances. I shove the door closed with the heel of my boot, locking us in with the turncoat.

"Mason, what—" the traitor starts, but I cut him off with an icy glare, the kind that used to freeze men in their tracks on the battlefield.

"Shut up, John!" I slam my palms on the desk, leaning into his space. "You're done."

Olivia stares incredulously. Her corporate mask slips, revealing the vulnerable woman beneath—a woman yearning for release, for the freedom to let go.

"I know everything," I say, my eyes never leaving his face. But it's Olivia I'm speaking to, and when I turn to look at her, her green eyes are wide, pupils dilated. "Trust me," I whisper and she nods, a silent surrender that ignites a fire within me. I can feel the heat radiating off her and smell the soft scent of her perfume mixing with the leather of the opulent office.

· · ·

"What the fuck, John? We were brothers ... you almost got us killed."

"It's just business Mason, just business," His words a blur, meaningless drivel of excuses and pleads. I don't care. I'm already thinking about how I'll strip away the layers of control from Olivia after this is done. How I'll make her mine in every way that counts.

5

———

MELTING ICE

"**W**hat are you waiting for, Mason?" I snap, my voice authoritative. The desire is now building inside me like a raging inferno. "Fuck me or get out." The police has arrested John and his accomplices and we are now alone.

"Come here," he orders.

He grabs my hips roughly, his hands moving up my skirt, up my thighs. He grips the lace of my panties and rips them apart, discarding them onto the floor. A moan escapes my lips as his fingertips trace the sensitive skin between my thighs.

"Oh, fuck... right there," I gasp, my fingers gripping the edge of the desk.

• • •

He doesn't disappoint; his fingers are going fast and rough, which is exactly how I like it. I tilt my head back, eyes closing in ecstasy.

Suddenly, he stops, leaving me aching. "Bastard!" I growl.

"I want you naked, begging for me," he commands. "Do it. Keep your shoes on." I take my shirt and bra off. I step forward, my high heels clicking against the marble floor.

He unzips his trousers, revealing the hard length that awaits me. "On your knees, Red," he says as he bends me over, his voice dripping with desire and power, slamming me down on his cock from behind. I gasp, my nails digging into the leather of the couch. He's so big, stretching me in ways I didn't know possible.

"Is this what you want, Olivia?" he growls in my ear, his voice a low, deep growl that sets my insides on fire. "You want me to take control?"

"Yes!" I whimper, my usual composure melting away as pleasure courses through my veins.

"You want me to fuck you hard?"

"Yes, yyyyyyeeee -ssss!!"

. . .

He grins wolfishly, his icy blue eyes alight with dominance. "I knew it. You've been begging for this, haven't you? Begging for someone to make you feel something other than ice?"

His words cut me to the core, but I don't deny them. Instead, I arch my back, silently begging for more. He takes my hips, bruising them as he pistons into me relentlessly.

"That's it, baby," he pants, his grip on my hipbones tightening. "Let go. I've got you."

And at that moment, as he claims me over and over again, I let go. I let go of my carefully constructed walls, pride, and fears. Because in his arms, in this moment, I can be weak.

"Mason," I moan, my orgasm building in my core, threatening to consume me whole. "I'm... I'm..."

"I know," he soothes, his voice a balm to my frayed nerves. "I've got you, Red."

The next thing I know, my world explodes into a million pieces. I'm crying out his name as my climax rips through me, taking everything I am and everything I thought I knew about myself with it.

EPILOGUE

I can't believe it's been five years since that fateful day. My life, once ruled by spreadsheets and boardroom battles, has been forever changed by one dominant, blue-eyed man.

Mason Reed.

As I sit at my desk, signing off on the final merger documents, my thoughts drift to the naughty weekend we have planned. A slow smile creeps onto my lips.

The click of heels on the marble floor snaps me out of my reverie. Gert, my ever-efficient assistant, steps inside my office. "Olivia, Mr. Reed is here."

"Send him in, Gert. And hold my calls for the next hour."

. . .

Mason strides in, his muscular frame filling the doorframe. Seeing him in his impeccable suit and tie makes my heart skip a beat. He's the picture of control and composure, but I know the beast that lurks underneath.

"Red," he says, his icy blue eyes raking over my crisp, white blouse and form-fitting skirt.

"Close the door," I say, my voice taking on a huskier, more commanding edge.

"Pardon?"

"Sorry," I hush, "Please close the door,"I ask softly this time.

"Better," he replies as he locks the door behind him and stands in front of my desk, the tension between us palpable. "What can I do for you, Olivia?"

I stand, my heels clicking on the marble floor as I walk toward him. "I need a little... stress relief," I purr, running my manicured nail down his immaculately pressed shirt.

Mason's eyes darken, and a predatory smirk curves his lips. "As you wish, Red."

. . .

With confident strides, he moves to the far end of my spacious office and retrieves a black leather bag I didn't even know was there. My heart races in anticipation as he unzips it.

"Strip," he commands.

With trembling fingers, I undress to my undies, my clothes pooling at my feet. I feel exposed and vulnerable, yet eager for what is to come. Mason doesn't crack a smile as he guides me in front of the glass window overlooking the bustling cityscape.

"Bend over," he growls, his voice rough with lust.

Without hesitation, I obediently fold over my sleek, mahogany desk, my heart pounding in anticipation. I feel the cool leather against my naked skin, sending shivers down my spine. Mason's strong hands massage my curves, every touch setting my skin on fire. Slowly, he wields the whip, teasingly tracing it down my spine before delivering a sharp slap across my bottom.

"Oh!" I gasp, the stinging pain sending a jolt of electricity straight to my core. He doesn't relent, alternating between caresses and light strokes of the whip, each impact leaving a delicious trail of heat in its wake. My mascara runs down my flushed cheeks, smudging my usually flawless makeup. I don't care. I can only think about the delicious tension coiling low in my belly, aching for release.

. . .

"Touch yourself," he growls, his voice thick with desire. "I want to see you come apart, Olivia."

I slip a trembling finger between my slick folds. Mason's eyes burn into mine, his desire evident in the way his jaw clenches. I moan, the sound bouncing off the walls of my pristine office as I edge closer and closer to climax. "Mason! I'm... I'm...!"

With a final, hard swat of the whip, I fly over the edge, my back arching as I cry out his name. Wave after wave of pleasure washes over me, rendering me boneless against the cool glass.

I can feel his throbbing erection. "I love you," he growls into my ear, his voice a low rumble of satisfaction and possession.

"I love you too," I pant, turning to meet his icy blue eyes. I can see my own reflection in them, a changed woman.

As I comply, he strips away my ruined panties and unzips his fly. "You're mine, Red," he grunts, guiding his thick length to my slick entrance.

"Yes, Mason, I'm yours," I pant, the admission spurring him on.

. . .

He penetrates me in one hard thrust, filling me completely, claiming me as his own. His hips slap against my ass in a primal rhythm, and I grip the edge of the desk for support.

"Say it again," he demands, his grip on my hip bruising.

"I'm yours!" I cry out, my backside stinging as his hand comes down on it with a resounding smack.

"Say it louder!"

"I'm yours, Mason!" I scream, my climax barreling towards me like a freight train.

With a final, earth-shattering thrust, he growls in my ear, "Say it!"

"I'm yours, Mason Reed! I'm yours!"

As our orgasms crash over us in a tidal wave of pleasure, I know that I've never been more mine than when I'm his. Mrs Reed.

GET YOUR FREE EBOOK

Sign up the Laura (L.A.) Mariani mailing list for a FREE steamy romance.

You'll be the first to hear about new releases, exclusive offers, bonus content and all Laura's news. You can even email her back. She loves chatting with her readers!

To claim your free ebook visit:
https://laura-mariani-author.ck.page/freeshortstory

ABOUT THE AUTHOR

Laura Alexandra (L.A.) Mariani is a best selling author of Short & Steamy Romance | Where Alpha Males Meet Fierce Heroines for Sweet Endings, your go-to author for captivating romance tales that will sweep you off your feet and keep you on the edge of your seat!

When Laura is not weaving stories of love, desire and suspense, you'll find her exploring the vibrant streets of London, drawing inspiration from its hidden corners and bustling markets, or strolling through the charming streets of Paris, savoring street food in Rome, or relaxing on a sun-kissed beach in Bali, her journeys fuelling her creativity and infuse her stories with wanderlust.

You can also follow her on

AUTHOR'S NOTE

Thank you so much for reading **The Bad Girl.**

I hope you enjoyed the story. A review would be much appreciated as it helps other readers discover the story. Or a few stars perhaps - the more the better ;-) !

Thanks.

Laura xx

9 781917 104173